VICTORY ★ SCHOOL SUPERSTARS

STONE ARCH BOOKS
a capstone imprint

Nobody Wants to Play with a Ball Hog

by Julie Gassman

illustrated by Jorge Santillan

Sports Illustrated KIDS

STONE ARCH BOOKS
a capstone imprint

VICTORY SCHOOL SUPERSTARS

Sports Illustrated KIDS *Nobody Wants to Play with a Ball Hog*
is published by Stone Arch Books — A Capstone Imprint
151 Good Counsel Drive, P.O. Box 669
Mankato, Minnesota 56002
www.capstonepub.com

Art Director and Designer: Bob Lentz
Creative Director: Heather Kindseth
Production Specialist: Michelle Biedscheid

Timeline photo credits: Shutterstock/Beth Van Trees
(top left); Sports Illustrated/Bob Rosato (bottom right),
Hy Peskin (top right), Manny Millan (middle left & bottom
left), Robert Beck (middle right).

Library of Congress Cataloging-in-Publication Data is
available on the Library of Congress website.

ISBN: 978-1-4342-2056-1 (library binding)
ISBN: 978-1-4342-2806-2 (paperback)

Summary: Because Tyler can't miss a shot when he plays
basketball, he quits throwing to his teammates.

Printed in the United States of America in Stevens Point, Wisconsin.
072011   006298R

TABLE OF CONTENTS

TYLER TROFEE

AGE: 10   **SPORT:** Basketball

SUPER SPORTS ABILITY: Super shooting makes Tyler a perfect shot.

VICTORY

21

VICTORY SCHOOL SUPERSTARS

CARMEN

DANNY

KENZIE

JOSH

ALICIA

TYLER

TYLER

Star Shooter

RIIINNNNNG!

Yes! That is the last bell of the day. It's time for basketball practice, the first one of the season. I have been looking forward to this day for weeks. Ever since I became Tyler Trofee, Star Shooter.

I will never forget the day I discovered my super skill. I was outside shooting baskets with my dad. We played a game of H-O-R-S-E. To play, I would take a shot. If I made it, Dad would have to shoot from the same place. Dad was just one shot away from losing, when he missed his last try.

"That's H-O-R-S-E, Dad. Sorry, but I win," I said.

"That was some great shooting," said Dad. "I don't think you missed one shot."

"Thanks, I have been practicing," I said.

"Show me what else you've got," said Dad.

I lazily tossed the ball toward the basket. I didn't put in much effort, so I didn't expect it to go through the hoop. But it did!

"You didn't even try, and it still went in," said Dad. "Try another one."

I walked back to the end of the driveway.
If this were a real basketball court, I would
be behind the three-point line. I took my
shot. *Swoosh!*

Then I started taking all sorts of crazy shots. I shot from behind my back. I shot using the backside of my hands, rather than my palms. I laid down flat on the ground and shot from there. Every one of my goofy shots went right through the hoop.

"I can't believe it. It's like I can't miss," I told my dad.

"You're right! No matter where you shoot from, it sails through," said Dad. "Tyler, do you know what this means?"

I gave Dad a confused look. I didn't know what he was getting at.

Finally he said, "I think you might have a super skill."

Sports School

I couldn't believe it. If what my dad said was right, if I really did have a super skill, I was in for big changes.

I had just heard about this cool school. It was called the Victory School for Super Athletes. I love basketball, so going to a sports school sounded awesome. There was a catch, though.

All the students at Victory have super skills. If they are great jumpers, they can soar fifty feet into the air. If they are fast runners, they can run a hundred meters in six seconds. I couldn't do anything like that.

But everything changed that day out on the driveway.

"Do you really think so, Dad?" I asked. "Do you think this is a super skill?"

"Yeah, I do," said Dad. "Anybody who makes shots like that must be a super shooter."

"Do you know what this means?" I asked.

"It means I need to make a phone call," said Dad.

"What? To who?" I ask.

"To that school you've been telling me and Mom about," said Dad. "I think you might have what it takes to be a Victory Superstar."

Our First Practice

Now here I am, practicing for the first time as a Superstar. After warm-ups and a few drills, Coach Murphy splits us into two teams.

"We are going to scrimmage," he says. "That means we will play for practice."

The other team wins the tip-off, so we all run toward their basket. I block a pass and grab the basketball. Then I take it down court and make an easy layup.

I am a pretty good rebounder, so I end up with the ball a lot. And every time I get the ball, I shoot. And every time I take a shot, I make it.

There are only a few seconds left on the clock, and I have the ball. I look and see a teammate alone under the basket. I could pass it his way, but it is more fun to score than it is to pass.

Even though I am a few feet behind the three-point line, I take the shot. It is a long way, but I know I will make it.

"Yes!" I shout. My side has won, 23 to 15. And I scored 18 of those points!

I go to give my teammates high fives, but they all act like they don't see me.

"All right guys, that's it. Good practice," says Coach Murphy. "Tyler, can you come over here for a minute?"

"What's up?" I ask.

"That was some great shooting out there, but I didn't see much passing," says Coach.

"Well, I know if I just shoot, I'll make it," I say.

"Basketball is a team sport. Right now, you are not playing with your team," says Coach.

"Well, my team won, and I'm sure they are happy about that," I say.

"I'm not so sure," he says. "Look, I have to get going. But next time, I want to see more passing and less shooting, Tyler."

"Okay," I agree, even though I don't really understand what the problem is.

Game
Time

After two weeks of practice, we will play our first game today. Practices haven't been as much fun as I thought they would be. Coach is always on my case to pass more. But I don't see why I need to be a better passer when I am a perfect shooter.

I've made some good friends in my classes, but most of the guys on the basketball team don't talk to me. I guess they are jealous of my super shooting. I bet they will be happy after I win this game for the Superstars.

As the game starts, I feel excited. Now is my chance to prove that I am a good guy to have on the team. I take my first shot. *Swoosh!*

Every shot I take goes through the hoop. At the end of the quarter, we are ahead by eight points. I grin at my teammates, but they look past me.

I try not to let them bother me. At the start of the second quarter, I come out ready for more of my shooting.

But something has changed. Now the two tallest players from the other side are guarding me. I can't even see around them. And I can't shoot.

Going into the half, we are behind by
nine points. I can't believe it. How did they
stop my super shooting?

Back in the locker room, Coach tells me,
"Tyler, they are on to you. I am sorry, but
you will need to sit out for the rest of the
game. They figured out how to stop you."

I can't believe this. It is the first game, and I only got to play half of it.

I watch the rest of the game from the bench. The only thing that makes me feel worse than being benched is when we lose the game.

Help from a Friend

"Hey, Tyler, wait up," yells a voice
behind me.

I don't want to talk to anybody, but I
turn around and see my friend Carmen.

"Hi, Carmen. How's it going?" I ask.

"It's probably better for me than it is for you. I'm sorry about the game," she says.

"Yeah, well, it's just one game. We'll win next time," I say.

"I noticed you sat out the second half of the game. You aren't hurt, are you?" she asks.

"No, Coach took me out since they stopped my shooting," I admit.

"They were sure guarding you hard," says Carmen, who plays basketball herself.

"I know! I can't miss, but that doesn't matter if I can't even shoot," I say.

"No offense, but why didn't you pass the ball more? There were a few guys open under the hoop," she says.

"There were?" I ask. "I guess I didn't notice them."

"When you have a super skill, you just want to show it off all the time. At least I do," says Carmen. I nod in agreement.

"But my coach says if we all just think about our own talents, we won't win," she continues. "It takes the whole team. You have to work together."

"Okay, okay, I get it," I snap. I don't really like hearing what Carmen has to say. I know she is right. But it is kind of embarrassing having one of your friends point out how you messed up.

"Sorry, it's none of my business," she says. Carmen looks really upset, and now I feel even worse.

"I'm sorry, Carmen," I say.

"Oh, that's okay. I'm always crabby after a loss too," she says.

"You're right. I haven't been playing with my team," I say. "And nobody wants to play with a ball hog. What do you think I should do? To get better, I mean."

"What we all have to do to get better: practice," she says. "And if I were you, I would make sure to keep an eye out for Kevin."

"Why Kevin?" I ask.

"Don't you know? He has the perfect super skill for a teammate like you. He never misses a pass, no matter how terrible it is," she says, laughing.

Back on the Court

After a week of countless passing drills, I am warming up for our second game of the season. Over the past seven days, I've worked on bounce passes, overhead passes, and chest passes. My teammates can tell I am trying, and I've even become friends with some of them.

Even though I've been practicing, a lot of my passes miss the mark. They are too high, too low, or too short. I am nervous about the game. If the other team stops my shooting and if I can't pass well, I might end up on the bench again for most of the game.

The game is about to begin when my teammate Kevin nudges me. "So you know how you have trouble with your passing?" he asks.

"Yeah," I say.

"Here's what you do," he says. "When you pass the ball, just imagine that the person you are passing to is actually a hoop."

"You think that would work?" I ask.

"I don't know, but it is worth a try," he says.

We win the tip-off, and I run downcourt. The point guard passes me the ball. I look to the basket, but two guys are guarding me. I can't shoot.

Then I see my teammate Charlie is wide open. It would be a long pass for me, but I remember what Kevin said. I picture a hoop right in front of Charlie and throw it his way. It works! Charlie easily catches my pass.

For the rest of the game, I keep shooting at the hoop. Of course, sometimes it's the real hoop. But a lot of times it is just the one in my head, the one I keep picturing in front of my teammates.

It turns out that playing with a team is always more fun than being a ball hog. And it works too. We just got our first win of the season!

SUPERSTAR OF THE WEEK
Tyler Trofee

Tyler Trofee is one of the newest students at Victory. He's put in a lot of hard work to become a better teammate. We took notice and made him our Superstar of the Week.

Tyler, you just recently discovered that you have a super talent. What was that like?
I was so pumped! But I don't think I was really used to it before I started on a new team. Most of the kids at school have known about their super skills for years, but I'm still just figuring mine out.

Is Victory everything you expected it to be?
Yeah! Everyone I know is into sports. It's pretty great!

What do you do when you're not at school or practice?
I have a lot of energy, so I like to ride my bike and skateboard around town. I usually bring my dog with me. In the summer, I hang out at the pool. I love the high dive.

You have a dog, huh? What kind?
She's a golden retriever. Her name is Maddy.

GLOSSARY

confused (kuhn-FYOOZD)—unable to understand

embarrassing (em-BA-ruhss-ing)—something that makes you feel awkward and uncomfortable

jealous (JEL-uhss)—wanting what someone else has

layup (LAY-uhp)—a shot made with one hand, from near a basket

lazily (LAYZ-eh-lee)—without much work or effort

point guard (POINT GARD)—the player responsible for bringing the ball down the court and setting up plays

rebounder (REE-bown-dur)—someone who catches a basketball after it has bounced off the basket

scrimmage (SKRIM-ij)—a game played for practice

three-point line (THREE-point LINE)—a curved line on a basketball court; shots made from behind this line are worth three points.

tip-off (TIP-awf)—the start of a basketball game; in a tip-off an official tosses the ball up between two players who jump and try to tap it to a teammate.

victory (VIK-tuh-ree)—a win in a game or contest

BASKETBALL IN HISTORY

1891 Dr. James Naismith invents basketball. The game uses two big **baskets** instead of the hoops we use today.

1895 Backboards are added behind the baskets. They stop fans on balconies from reaching over and helping their teams.

1906 Baskets with holes in the bottom are used for the first time.

1949 The **National Basketball Association (NBA)** is formed.

1960 Danny Heater of West Virginia scores 135 points in a high school game. He holds a world record for most points scored in a game.

1992 The **"Dream Team"** wins the Olympic gold medal.

1997 The **Women's National Basketball Association (WNBA)** is formed.

2003 NBA star **Michael Jordan** retires. He led the Chicago Bulls to six championships.

2008 The **Boston Celtics** win their 17th NBA championship. The team has won more championships than any other team.

VICTORY SCHOOL SUPERSTARS

Read them ALL!

STONE ARCH BOOKS
a capstone imprint